Bright ≡Summaries.com

The Confessions (books I-IV)

BY JEAN-JACQUES ROUSSEAU

Written by Sabrina Zoubir
Translated by Oliver Brown

The Confessions (books I-IV)

BY JEAN-JACQUES ROUSSEAU

Bright
≡Summaries.com

JEAN-JACQUES ROUSSEAU

Geneva-based writer, philosopher and musician

- **Born in 1712 in Geneva**

- **Died in 1778 at Ermenonville**

- **Some of his works:**

    - *Julie or the New Heloise* (1761), epistolary novel

    - *Émile ou De l'éducation* (1762), treatise on education

    - *Les Rêveries du promeneur solitaire* (between 1776 and 1778), a philosophical reflection

Jean-Jacques Rousseau is one of the most famous thinkers of the Enlightenment and one of the spiritual fathers of the French Revolution. Born in Geneva in 1712, he had an eventful youth during which he worked in various professions, including tutoring and being a copyist. In Paris, Rousseau became involved with the philosophers of the Enlightenment and gained fame in 1750 with his *Discours sur les sciences et les arts*, in which he developed what was to become the central theme of his thinking: man is naturally born good and happy, it is society that corrupts him and makes him unhappy. This was followed by major works such as *Du contrat social* (1762) and *Émile ou De l'éducation* (1762). Considered subversive, they were quickly condemned and banned. Rousseau was then forced into a series of exiles that kept him away from France until 1769. Suffering from a sense of persecution, he devoted the last part of his life to autobiographical works: *Les Confessions* (written in 1765-1767), and *Les Rêveries du promeneur solitaire* (written between 1776 and 1778). He died in isolation in 1778.

THE CONFESSIONS (BOOKS I-IV)

An autobiography of an Enlightenment philosopher.

- **Genre:** autobiography

- **Reference edition:** *Les Confessions* (Livres I-IV), Paris, Gallimard, coll. "Folio classique", 1997, 272 p.

- **1re edition:** 1782

- **Themes:** loneliness, sadness, emotion, life, memory, nature, psychology

Rousseau's *Confessions* is a posthumously published autobiographical work, the first six books of which were written between 1765 and 1767 and the last six in 1769 and 1770. It covers the first 53 years of his life. The idea of writing his confessions had its roots in a particular context. Indeed, by denouncing in *Emile* the bad influence of political and religious power on education, he attracted the wrath of the French, Swiss and Dutch authorities. They considered his theories indecent, and in 1762 ordered the book to be publicly burned and the author condemned. Rousseau was banned from these countries and went into exile in Neuchâtel. Barely two years later, Voltaire accused him of having written a moralistic treatise on education while he had abandoned his four children to public assistance. Betrayed by the accusation of his former friend, Rousseau felt sullied and decided, in an almost compulsive desire to justify himself, to write his *Confessions*.

SUMMARY

BOOK I – 0-16 YEARS (1712 – MARCH 1728)

Rousseau begins by recounting his birth in Geneva in 1712 and the death of his mother following childbirth. The young Jean-Jacques was left alone with his father, with whom he spent long nights reading. These readings shaped the young boy's mind and he discovered the great authors and an astonishing range of feelings ("I had no idea of things, that all feelings were already known to me", p. 37). However, Rousseau's father went abroad and entrusted his son to the pastor Lambercier. In Bossey, Jean-Jacques experienced his first sexual feelings thanks to the spankings of Mlle Lambercier, but he also discovered the feeling of injustice with the episode of the broken comb (at the origin of his profound revulsion against injustice). In 1724, he returned to his uncle's house in Geneva for a few months, before beginning his apprenticeship: first with Mr Masseron (clerk), then with Mr Ducommun (engraver), both of whom were contemptuous and tyrannical towards him. These unfortunate experiences develop certain vices in him that lead the young apprentice to lie and steal.

A few years later, when he returned from a walk in the countryside, Rousseau found the city gates closed. He saw this as a sign of fate and chose to leave Geneva for good.

BOOK II – THE YEAR OF HIS 16TH BIRTHDAY (MARCH – DECEMBER 1728)

Jean-Jacques begins an itinerant life: he wanders around Geneva and never ceases to be amazed by such beautiful nature. He met M. de Pontverre, a benevolent priest who advised him to go to Annecy to stay with a certain Mme de Warens (1700-1762). The young 16-year-old complies, far from suspecting how decisive this meeting will be for him. This woman, for whom he confessed to feeling an instant love, sent him to the hospice for catechumens in Turin, where he was sexually abused by a Moor. Once converted to Catholicism, he left the hospice without regret.

Wandering through the streets of Turin this time, he meets Mlle de Basile, with whom he has a brief and platonic love affair, and then she finds him a position as a lackey with the Countess of Vercellis. However, like a real rascal, Jean-Jacques steals a ribbon and brazenly accuses Marion, the maid, of having committed the theft. Dismayed, the poor girl bursts into tears, and her apparent weakness does her no credit in the face of Rousseau's "such diabolical audacity". In the end, they are both sent away and Jean-Jacques sets off on the road to his fate.

BOOK III – FROM 16 TO 18 YEARS (MARCH 1728 – APRIL 1730)

The vigour of his youth combined with the idleness he experiences on returning to his former hostess leads Jean-Jacques to practice exhibitionism. In search of a new home, he occasionally visits M. Gaime, an abbot from Savoy. In the course of their exchanges, Rousseau discovers and reflects on a whole host of philosophical notions. Then, thanks to the Count de la Roque, he became a lackey in a house of great renown, the home of the Count of Gouvon. At first disappointed to be a servant again, Jean-Jacques is nevertheless noticed for his intelligence and becomes the secretary of the latter. But despite this new position and his good understanding with the count, he has only one idea in mind: to find Annecy and Mme de Warens. He is dismissed, then goes to her house unannounced.

Despite the young man's fears, Mme de Warens invites him to stay with her. This was the beginning of a long and tender complicity. During a seminar on music, he met M. Le Maitre, a musician with whom he later went to Lyon. The latter was epileptic and suffered a terrible seizure in the street. Giving in to panic, Rousseau abandoned him and ran away in a cowardly manner.

BOOK IV – FROM 18 TO 19 YEARS (APRIL 1730 – OCTOBER 1731)

Back in Annecy, Rousseau lives with Mr Venture. He thinks a lot about Mme de Warens, especially as he does not know where she is. Then he decides to leave to teach music in Lausanne, although he knows nothing about it. He found refuge in the inn of Mr Perrotet, to whom he pretended to be a composer and music teacher looking for an audience. The innkeeper promises to find him some students. Jean-Jacques soon becomes a 'master singer, without knowing how to decipher a tune' (p. 98). However, after a disastrous concert in which the mocking laughter of the audience is mixed with indignation, he breaks down and confesses his imposture to one of his symphonists. That evening, all of Lausanne is aware of his deception and, not very proud, he leaves the city.

During a stopover in Solothurn, he meets the Marquis de Bonac who takes him in and employs him, before helping him to leave for Paris. Finally disappointed by the idea he had of the capital, Jean-Jacques cannot help but return to Annecy when he learns of the return of Mme de Warens. As benevolent as ever towards his protégé, the latter finds him a position as secretary to the King of Piedmont-Sardinia. A new life begins for Rousseau.

CHARACTER STUDY

ROUSSEAU'S FAMILY

His Parents

Rousseau's mother, Suzanne Bernard, daughter of Minister Bernard, was a citizen of rather well-to-do social conditions. Isaac Rousseau, her father, was a watchmaker by trade and came from a much more modest family. For this reason, he takes some time before he succeeds in marrying Suzanne, with whom he is madly in love, and whom he has known since the age of eight. From their mutual love two children are born: a first son, François, and seven years later, a second, Jean-Jacques. Suzanne succumbs to a tragic fate and dies seven days after the birth of her last child. Devastated by grief, Jean-Jacques' father will never recover, unwittingly burdening his son with a double guilt. Isaac chooses to escape the sad reality through the books left by Suzanne. He takes Jean-Jacques on his literary journeys, and a tender complicity is born between father and son. However, this complicity ends rather quickly, since following a dispute with M. Gautier in 1722, Isaac goes into exile in Geneva, leaving Jean-Jacques under the care of his uncle, Gabriel Bernard.

Les Bernard

Rousseau was close to his aunt and uncle, but it was with his cousin that he shared the happiest moments of his childhood. He was one of the first people for whom he confessed to having real feelings: "Until then, I had only known high, but imaginary feelings. The habit of living together in a peaceful state unites me tenderly with my cousin Bernard." (p. 42). Together they spend nearly five unforgettable years boarding with the Lambercier family. Jean-Jacques describes their relationship as follows: "Our work, our amusements, our tastes were the same: we were alone, we were the same age, each of us needed a companion; to separate us was, in a way, to annihilate us." (p. 42).

Jean-Jacques

He is at the same time the main character of the *Confessions*, the narrator of the story and the author of the text; a peculiarity that can make the character difficult to grasp. From the outset, Rousseau clearly states his intention to "paint a man in all the truth of his nature", and indeed, the descriptions given are not always to his advantage. In an effort to be absolutely transparent, Rousseau reveals his weaknesses to the reader, talks about his failures in no uncertain terms, and confesses his moral faults. At the beginning of the *Confessions*, he draws the reader's pity by presenting himself as a sickly, almost handicapped child:

"I was born almost dying; there was little hope of preserving me. I brought with me the seed of an inconvenience which the years have strengthened, and which now sometimes gives me a break only to let me suffer more cruelly in another way." (p. 36).

This fragility seems to go hand in hand with the hypersensitivity he expresses, whether in contact with nature, women, or literature. In terms of his love affairs, for example, they are all as intense as they are platonic. Presumably, what he describes as a lack of success with women is actually a problem related to a confusion between his imagination and the real world. The reason for this is the impressive amount of reading material he absorbs from a young age. This forged his love of travel, his dreamy character and led to his social maladjustment. Deeply immersed in all these romantic stories, reality no longer lives up to his expectations, and he instinctively withdraws into himself and becomes solitary.

Yet all these fragile and sensitive aspects of his being form a strange contrast with some of the elements recounted in his stories. Indeed, despite his apparent shyness with women, he goes through a period of exhibitionism. Yet it is hard to imagine that a person who pretends to be reserved would be capable of lying so brazenly (when he accuses a servant girl of theft in front of an entire assembly or when he pretends to be a famous composer when he knows nothing about music). Is it madness or ambition? One thing is certain: through his choices, his risk-taking and his nerve, the complex character of Jean-Jacques commands admiration despite his flaws.

The Lambercier

Rousseau has only good memories of his years of apprenticeship with the pastor Lambercier, a "very reasonable man" (p. 42), who contributed to his gentle education.

The pastor's sister, Mlle Lambercier, teaches catechism. She is the guarantor of the mother's authority, but her severity does not prevent her from remaining fair or from showing the children all the affection they deserve. She is also the source of young Jean-Jacques' first sexual feelings. The passage describing the pleasure he feels when he is spanked by her is one of the best known extracts from the *Confessions*:

"For a long time she kept to the threat, and this threat of a punishment which was new to me seemed very frightening; but after the execution, I found it less terrible to the test than the expectation had been, and the strangest thing is that this punishment endeared me even more to the one who had imposed it on me [...]." (p. 44).

Mme de Warens

Mme de Warens is a noblewoman with an unfulfilled love life. Married at a young age to M. de Warens, of whom she had no children, she left her husband, her family and her town on a whim for a prince who eventually sent her to a convent. On this subject, Rousseau says that she made the choice to run away in a blunder similar to his, "and that she had plenty of time to cry too." (p. 84). For this young lady bears many similarities to Jean-Jacques: like him, she is impulsive and passionate, like him, she loses her mother at birth, and like him, she forges her education on the job, as she experiences it. When they met through M. de Pontverre, Rousseau is only 16 years old, and M. de Warens 28. It is undoubtedly the most decisive meeting in the author's life ("This period of my life decided my character", p. 84). The bond that unites them inspires him with "peace of heart, calm, serenity, security, assurance" (p. 87).

Also, there is no shortage of laudatory physical descriptions of this woman: "I see a face full of grace, beautiful blue eyes full of sweetness, a dazzling complexion, the contour of an enchanting throat." (pp. 83-84). Her voice makes Rousseau "tremble" (p. 84). Although his feelings for her may appear ambiguous in some of his sentences, what emerges above all from his descriptions is a deep admiration and respect. Moreover, he calls her "mummy" while she calls him "little".

The Abbot of Gaime

Abbé Gaime is another important character in the *Confessions*, because of the strong influence he exerts on the young Jean-Jacques, but also because he inspired the author to create the character of the Savoyard vicar. Jean-Jacques was eager to learn from him and liked to visit him, because what he learned from these talks was invaluable to him:

"With him I found advantages that have benefited me all my life, the lessons of sound morals and the maxims of right reason [...]. Mr Gaime took care to put me in my place and to show me to myself, without sparing me or discouraging me [...]. He gave me a true picture of human life, of which I had only false ideas." (p. 133).

READING KEYS

EMOTION AT THE HEART OF AN UNPRECEDENTED UNDERTAKING

Convinced that truth is to be sought in the hearts of men, Rousseau proposes himself as a subject of study. From the very first lines, he announces the unique character of his project: "I am forming an enterprise that has never had an example and whose execution will have no imitator." However, if it was he who made the autobiographical genre popular, *The Confessions* were inspired by a work of St Augustine (one of the Latin Church Fathers, 354-430), of the same title. Rousseau nonetheless gives a poignant account of the history of his personality. He reveals everything with a remarkable attention to detail, placing emotion at the heart of his accounts. His extensive reading is the source of this approach, prompting the observation that "I had no idea of things, that all feelings were already known to me." (p. 37).

Far from being pejorative, this predominance of the sensory is claimed by Rousseau and lies at the foundation of his philosophy: according to him, it is through sensation that we have access to truth, that is to say, to an understanding of the world and our deepest self. In this respect, *The Confessions* can be considered as a precursor of modern psychology: the analysis of oneself, of what one feels, allows us to know ourselves better and thus to go beyond the stage of suffering. Nevertheless, it should be pointed out that Rousseau's main aim is to help us move forward in the history of humanity: "I beseech you [...] not to destroy a unique and useful work, which can serve as a first comparison for the study of men." (p. 31).

STRATEGIC WRITING

On the assumption that Rousseau is trying to justify himself to his readers in relation to the accusations made against him, he sets up a whole strategy to obtain the reader's understanding, compassion, and indulgence. This strategy intervenes not only in the choice of the events he recounts, but also in the intimate style he adopts. As we have already pointed out, one of Rousseau's tactics to win over his reader is to arouse their pity, in order to better find their forgiveness. To this end, he places himself in the position of victim from the outset: "I was the sad fruit of this return" (about his birth), "I was born crippled and ill", "my birth was the first of my misfortunes" (p. 35), "I was born almost dying" (p. 36). He brings this victim status to bear by resorting to excessive hyperbole and thus chooses vocabulary and turns of phrase that tend to dramatise his stories to the maximum. He uses this same stylistic device to make the admission of his faults seem gentle (the theft of the ribbon, the pleasure experienced during Mlle Lambercier's spankings, the abandonment of his epileptic friend in the midst of a seizure): by magnifying his fault, when the punch line occurs, the reader's judgement unconsciously minimises the act in question, finding the author perhaps excessive.

Here, for example, are the few words he addresses to his reader before telling him the episode of the walnut tree: "O you readers curious about the great story of the walnut tree on the terrace, listen to the horrible tragedy and refrain from shuddering if you can! Yet it is only a minor lie, as children often tell, and of no real consequence."

In this respect, his various confessions are just as much a part of his writing strategy: by giving the impression of delivering an exhaustive account of his faults, including the most unmentionable ones, Rousseau is still trying to prove his innocence. If the things of which his detractors accuse him are not in his *Confessions*, then the reader will undoubtedly deduce that they are only rumours. As for the accusations made against him in this book, as we have just seen, the author will do everything in his power to justify himself and win the indulgence of the judging reader.

THE MULTIPLE ROLE OF READERS

With *The Confessions*, Rousseau attempts to establish a special relationship with his reader. He does not hesitate to interrupt his narrative regularly to address him indirectly: "As the reader progresses in my life, he will become aware of my moods, and he will feel all this without my dwelling on it" (p. 71), "Ah! let us not anticipate the miseries of my life; I will only occupy my readers too much with this sad subject" (p. 78), etc. In addition, we notice something completely new in the structure of the *Confessions*: the interaction that the author sets up between himself and his reader through the various roles that he imposes on him. The first function he gives him is that of friend and confidant. To this end, he tells his reader the story of his life in great detail, thus proving his unfailing confidence in him; he confesses everything, even the unmentionable. Moreover, beyond the confidences he delivers as one would with a close friend, by showing himself to be vulnerable (despite his great literary skill, which does not leave a well-informed audience fooled), he allows the common man to identify with him and invites him to feel closer to him. However, Rousseau does not only seek to win the friendship of his reader. In addition to witnessing the adventures that are told to him, the reader is faced with the difficult task of interpreting the story that is being told to him. This is how Rousseau expresses his will: "It is up to him to assemble these elements and to determine the being they compose: the result must be his work; and if he is mistaken, the error will be all his doing." (p. 230). In fact, the reader's main role is that of judge of the confessions: "Whether nature has done right or wrong in judging the mould into which she has thrown me, that is what can only be judged after reading me." (p. 33).

THE THEME OF NATURE

Nature is one of the essential themes in Rousseau's work. Far from being a simple setting, it had a saving effect on him, comforting him when he was in a bad way, accompanying him in all the stages of his life. In *The Confessions*, we see a real personification of nature, which, as a witness to the events of his life, appears almost as a friend, and sometimes even as a mother.

For the young Jean-Jacques, nature is also the ideal refuge. It allows him to give free rein to his imagination and to escape from the magnificent spectacle it offers to his senses.

However, the pleasure it gives him is not only cerebral, it is also physical. It should be remembered that Jean-Jacques discovered nature through long hours of walking. During his first twenty years, how many country walks did he take? How many times did he walk through France, Italy and Switzerland, often without even knowing where he was going? For him, nature is synonymous with freedom and the absence of constraints, and this is what reinforces the positive and enthusiastic feeling that it inspires in him.

FOOD FOR THOUGHT

A FEW QUESTIONS TO DEEPEN YOUR REFLECTION...

- What do you think are the limits of Rousseau's enterprise? Argue.

- In your opinion, why are the first four books of the *Confessions* more important than the other eight?

- What role did the *Confessions* play in the history of literature?

- What are the differences between autobiography and autofiction?

- "I feel my heart and I know men. I am not made like any of those I have seen; I dare to believe that I am not made like any of those who exist. If I am not better, at least I am different. Whether nature did right or wrong in breaking the mould into which she cast me, that is what can only be judged after reading me." List all the figures of speech you observe in this extract and comment on them.

- If you had to link *The Confessions* to a literary trend, which one would it be and why?

- What was meant by the term 'philosopher' in the 18th century? What role does it play? Can Rousseau be considered a philosopher?

- What is Rousseau's relationship with women? How do you explain this?

- How do the *Confessions* shed light on Rousseau's work?

TO GO FURTHER

REFERENCE EDITION

ROUSSEAU J.-J., *The Confessions* (Books I-IV), Paris, Gallimard, "Folio classique" collection, 1997.

Your opinion is important to us!
Leave a comment on the website of your online bookshop
and share your favourites on social networks!

Bright ≡Summaries.com

More guides to rediscover your love of literature

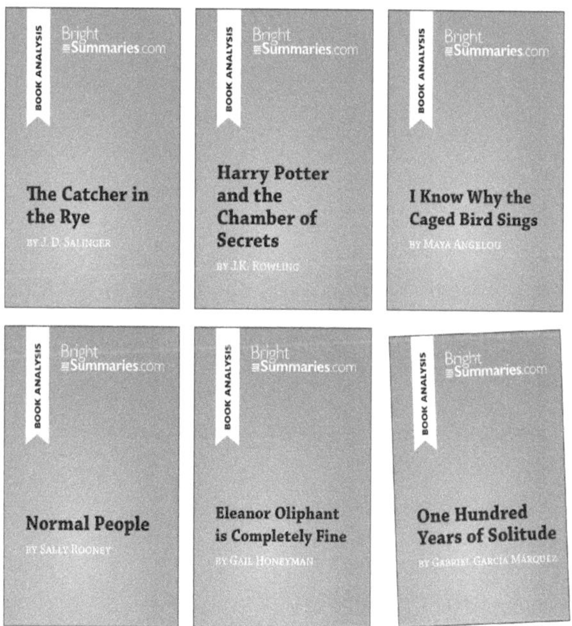

www.BrightSummaries.com

Ebook EAN: 9782808686600
Paperback EAN: 9782808698009
Legal Deposit: D/2023/12603/1080

Cover: © Primento
Digital conception by Primento, the digital partner of publishers.